Dracula

Bram Stoker

Simplified by John Turvey

Longman Group UK Limited,
Longman House, Burnt Mill, Harlow,
Essex CM20 2JE, England
and Associated Companies throughout the world.

This simplified edition © Longman Group UK Limited 1987

First published 1987

ISBN 0-582-52282-X

Set in 10/13 point Linotron 202 Versailles
Produced by Longman Group (FE) Limited
Printed in Hong Kong

Acknowledgements

'Photographs © BBC' 1977.

The cover background is a wallpaper design called NUAGE,
courtesy of Osborne and Little plc.

Stage 3: 1300 word vocabulary

Please look under *New words* at the back of this book
for explanations of words outside this stage.

Contents

Introduction

Bram Stoker

Bram Stoker (Bram is an unusual short form of Abraham) was born in Dublin and educated there. In 1866 he joined the Irish Civil Service, the people who worked for the government in all its offices and departments. It seemed a rather dull life, although he was interested enough to write some reports and books about subjects such as the work of the law courts. In 1878 he left the civil service and became the secretary, and later the manager, of Sir Henry Irving. Sir Henry was the most outstanding figure in the London theatres in the second half of the nineteenth century. He acted and also produced plays in the theatres.   His favourite plays were Shakespeare's; he was a famous Hamlet, Shylock (in *The Merchant of Venice*) and Malvolio (in *Twelfth Night*).   But Irving also enjoyed producing and playing in melodramas, plays which are too exciting to be believed.   They would include plays about frightening events like those in this book. Perhaps that is where Bram Stoker first found his interest in the vampire myths.

Dracula

Bram Stoker's *Dracula* appeared first in 1897. It caught the public interest at a time when the supernatural – ghost stories and accounts of events that cannot be explained – had come into fashion. It was an immediate success, and it was followed – and continues to be followed, thanks partly to films and television – by very many other stories about vampires and other "ghoulies and ghosties and long-legged beasties and things that go bump in the night".

Dracula was not the first story about the vampire myths. There had been many mentions of them, and Heinrich Marschner's opera *Der Vampyr* was popular in German opera houses long before 1897. For one more example, Lord Byron's story-poem *The Giaour* (1813) has the lines:

> But first on earth, as vampire sent,
> Thy corse[1] shall from its tomb be rent[2],
> Then ghastly[3] haunt[4] thy native place
> And suck the blood of all thy race.

([1]corpse, dead body; [2]torn; [3]in a terrifying way; [4]return to visit as a ghost)

and all his readers would have understood the reference.

But it is to *Dracula* that people turn for the full taste of the old myths. And it is the name "Dracula" that is known (with variations in pronunciation) in nearly every part of the world. The tape recording of this book, read by a well-known actor, will give you an idea of how exciting the story can sound.

Transylvania

The name comes from Latin words meaning "Beyond the forests", but it is a real country, not an imaginary one. It is actually in Romania today, lying between the west of Romania and the south of Hungary. It is a mountainous country, enclosed on the east and south by the Carpathian Mountains and the Transylvanian Alps, in the west by the Bihor Mountains. The people are of many origins, including the gipsies who play a part in the story.

Vampires

The belief in vampires is a very ancient one, most of all in the Slavonic countries such as Transylvania. Perhaps the stories came from much further east, like the Slavonic people themselves and their languages. In the stories, the vampire was the ghost of a dead wrongdoer. The ghost returned from the grave in the shape of a huge bat and fed on the blood of sleeping people. These people usually became vampires themselves. So long as it could get human blood in this way, the vampire would never die.

When Christianity came to the Slavs, the old beliefs did not end immediately. But people added the protection of the new religion to the old beliefs in the protective power of certain plants, especially garlic, and of fire. They still believed that the only way to kill a vampire (and set its spirit – in Christian times its soul – free) was to drive a sharpened length of wood through its heart, but Christianity gave the simple people the added strength of the cross, the name of God, and the bread that a priest had blessed in church.

Chapter 1
Castle Dracula

Everything in Transylvania seemed very strange to Jonathan Harker. There was so much to tell Mina, the girl he was going to marry.

There were mountains, thick forests, and fast-flowing rivers. Castles stood on high rocks, and he hoped that Castle Dracula would be like them. The people were strange too; they were very kind and polite, but when he told them that he was going to see Count Dracula, they were afraid. At Bistritz the hotel keeper's wife had given him a cross.

"Please take it," she said. "There is danger at Castle Dracula."

Count Dracula's own carriage came to take him on the last part of the journey through the darkness. As the carriage climbed into the mountains, Jonathan saw the red eyes of wolves all round the carriage. And when the wolves came too close, the driver shouted at them as if they were his own dogs.

The carriage left Jonathan standing in front of a huge, old door strengthened with iron. He could see no windows on the ground floor, but a light above showed that the castle was not empty. There was no bell, so he could only wait until somebody let him in.

He stood some minutes listening to the wolves before he heard a noise from the other side of the door. It opened, and there stood a tall, dark-haired man, dressed in black and holding a silver lamp. He smiled, and said:

"I offer my house to you. Come freely, go safely, and leave something of the happiness you bring."

1

"Count Dracula?" asked Jonathan, as he shook a strong, cold hand.

"I am Dracula, and I am glad, Mr Harker, to have you in my house. I will carry your bags – it is late, and my servants are not up."

Taking the lamp, Jonathan followed him up the stairs, and across a large, well-lit room (where he was pleased to see a big wood fire and a table spread for a meal) to a bedroom.

The count did not join him at the table. He said he had already eaten. So while Jonathan ate, the count read the letter that Jonathan had brought from old Mr Hawkins, the lawyer he worked for. He seemed pleased, and handed it back at last to Jonathan so that he could read the good things that Mr Hawkins had said about him.

After dinner they sat talking by the fire. Jonathan was glad that the count spoke good English, and the count seemed glad to have someone to talk English to. It was he who had most to say, which gave Jonathan a chance to study his face.

It was an unusual face: a strong, well-shaped nose, very pointed ears, red lips and sharp, white teeth. But the most noticeable thing about him was his unnatural paleness. He must have been old, and yet seemed strong and active. Jonathan also noticed his hands, which had hair growing on the insides, and fingers that were long and sharp at the ends. He did not like it when the count, while talking, sometimes touched his arm. Also the smell of the count's breath made him feel ill. It was the smell of death! "Is this why the people feared him?" Jonathan wondered.

Silence fell in the castle at last, but outside the wolves could still be heard. "My children are excited tonight. We

2

have few visitors," the count said. He rose. It was getting light, and the first night at Castle Dracula was over.

Jonathan was tired and slept late. He walked into the room where he had eaten the night before and found breakfast laid, and a coffee pot standing near the fire. Now he could see what Castle Dracula really looked like: old, rather worn and dusty. But the coffee pot from which he was pouring himself coffee was of gold.

When he had eaten he looked for a bell to let the servants know they could take the plates away, but there was no bell, and there were no servants. At least, there were no servants in the part of the castle where he found he could go. Many doors were locked.

One door that was not locked opened into a sitting room containing books, and he was surprised to find English books and newspapers among them. He sat down to read, and was still sitting there that evening when the count entered.

"I am glad you have found your way here," he said. "Since I decided to buy a house in England I have tried to learn something about English life. I am sorry that I only know the language from books, but I hope by talking to you, Mr Harker, to learn it better. That is why I hope you will not want to leave my castle very soon.

"And while you are here," he went on, "remember my house is yours. Go anywhere you wish, except where the doors are locked. And there, of course, you will not wish to go. There are reasons for these things; we are in Transylvania, and Transylvania is not England." He showed his teeth in a wolf-like smile.

"Now, tell me something about the house that your Mr Hawkins has bought for me. There will be some papers I

Count Dracula reads the letter from Mr Hawkins

must put my name to. Naturally I wish to know every-thing."

"First," replied Jonathan, "I hope you will find that the house is what you really want. To tell you the truth, it's not the kind of house that most people want, but it *is* what you asked for.

"The house is called Carfax. It has a lot of land, most of it covered by trees, which make it rather dark. The house itself is large and old, with few windows. Next to it, and part of it, is an old, disused church. I am afraid you will not have much company at Carfax, because there are not many houses near – your only neighbour is a doctor in charge of a hospital for mad people."

"I am glad the house is old," replied the count. "I come from an old family and do not like to live in a house without history. Nor do I mind the darkness. For a man who is old, and alone, and thinks much about the dead, darkness is nothing to fear."

He wrote his name on the papers and led the way into the dining room, where dinner was waiting. Again he did not eat, saying that he had eaten out that day.

That evening and the following ones passed in the same way as the first. Although Jonathan found it unnatural to talk by night and sleep by day, it seemed to be what the count was used to, and he felt he ought to please him. As for the count, he behaved pleasantly and was always interesting, but for some unknown reason Jonathan was afraid of him. It was not only the look that he sometimes caught in his strangely red eyes. It was a feeling that the count was no ordinary man – that he had unnatural powers.

It was one day about a week after his arrival that

Jonathan first had proof of this. He was standing by his window, shaving in front of the little looking glass which Mina, luckily, had given him – luckily, because there was no looking glass in his room, nor in any other room of the castle.

Suddenly he felt the touch of a hand and heard a voice wish him good morning. The count was standing by his side. Jonathan jumped. The count was a quiet walker, and could have entered the room unheard – but hardly unseen.

"Why didn't I see him in the looking glass?" thought Jonathan. "He is standing in front of it even now, but although I can see myself I can't see him."

As Jonathan continued to stare into the looking glass he noticed that he had cut himself. A little stream of blood was flowing down his neck. He looked at the count again to make sure that he really was in the room, and froze with fear! Dracula was watching the blood as it ran down his neck, watching like a hungry animal. He looked as if he was going to attack him!

The blood had by this time almost reached the cross which the woman at the hotel had given him. Without thinking, Jonathan rubbed the blood away with the back of his hand, lifting the cross as he did so. The count's face changed. He looked like a madman. For some time he stood there shaking, as if wanting to attack him but somehow unable to. Suddenly he picked up the looking glass and threw it out of the window. In the long silence that followed, Jonathan found himself counting the time before he heard the crash on the rocks below. The count turned:

"The Devil gave looking glasses to make men proud. I do not allow them in my house," he said. And then as he left: "Try not to cut yourself. It is more dangerous in this

7

Dracula tells Jonathan he does not allow looking glasses

country than you think."

At first Jonathan could only stand there with the soap drying on his face, unable to do anything. Why is the man so excited by blood? What kind of man is it who can't be seen in a looking glass?

He looked down from the window. The looking glass must have fallen a hundred metres before it hit the ground. How hard it would be to escape from this castle. Thoughts of locked doors passed through his mind. Jonathan began to wonder. Was he Count Dracula's visitor – or his prisoner?

Chapter 2
The three women

Jonathan's study of the law had taught him to face facts, and the facts showed that he was some kind of prisoner. But surely only for a few more days. And if Dracula frightened him, this did not necessarily mean that he was in danger. He must hide his thoughts and try to learn more.

That evening he heard the count enter. Noticing that he did not come straight to the sitting room, Jonathan went quietly to the door of his own room and saw the count making the bed. When later he saw him laying the table in the dining room something, at least, became clear. There were no servants in the castle. It was the count himself who did all the work and drove the carriage. Jonathan was alone in the castle with Dracula!

Alone? But no, not quite alone, as he found out a few days later.

Time passed as before. Jonathan got up late, breakfasted and read in the sitting room. At night he listened to the count talking about the history of his family and of his country. This was nearly the same thing, because the Draculas had been at the centre of all the happenings that formed the history of Transylvania. Here he was interesting, and told his stories with such feeling that one might think he had been present at the battles he talked about.

Sometimes he talked about more ordinary things: about England, law, ships and trains. And Jonathan was surprised to know how much he had learned. He seemed interested in sending goods to England and wanted to find a town by the sea where they could be sent.

"I do not want a big town where there might be trouble and waste of time. What do you think, Mr Harker?"

"Why not Whitby?" said Jonathan, thinking of Mina and her beautiful friend Lucy, who were going on holiday to that fine old north-eastern fishing town. He told the count about the town – and also about Mina. The count was interested. Whitby seemed suitable. He also said how happy he was that Jonathan was going to be married, and gave him his best wishes. Pleased by his interest, Jonathan took out photographs of Mina and Lucy. The count smiled.

"What pretty girls!" he said in a voice that made Jonathan wish he had not been so ready to show his photographs. "Your Miss Mina – she will surely want to know how you are. And Mr Hawkins, too. Have you written to them since you arrived?"

"I have not had much chance of sending letters," Jonathan replied.

"Then write now, my good friend. Write to Mr Hawkins and tell him that you will stay with me for another month."

Jonathan's heart grew cold. "Do you want me to stay so long?"

"I wish it. You were sent to look after my business, and my business makes it necessary for you to be here some time longer."

Jonathan now felt even more like a prisoner than ever. "How can I go on living at the castle for another month? Yet what can I do?" he thought. "I work for Mr Hawkins, and Count Dracula is paying for my services."

The count continued: "I ask you not to write about anything but business in your letters – except to say that you are well." He then handed Jonathan paper and envelopes of the thinnest kind. Anything he wrote could easily be read through these envelopes. So Jonathan sat down and wrote letters containing nothing of what he most wanted to tell. The count took them, and before he went said this: "Let me warn you, my young friend. If you leave these rooms and go into any other part of the castle, do not fall asleep there. The castle is old. Strange things have happened here, and bad dreams may come to you. In your own room you are safe."

"Safe!" thought Jonathan. "How I wish I could feel safe from you!"

He went down to the great door which opened on to the courtyard. It was locked as usual; the key must be in the count's room. One or two small rooms were open, but they led nowhere. And then he noticed a door at the end of a short passage. At first it seemed to be locked, but it had only dropped and was resting on the floor. By lifting and then pushing it he was able to make it open enough for him to pass through. Feeling his way up a dark stair he found himself in a pleasant moonlit room which seemed to be next to his own bedroom. From the furniture it looked as if it might long ago have been used by the ladies of the castle.

He hung out of the window enjoying the night air. Getting into a different part of the castle made him feel he had beaten Dracula in a small way.

Just then a sound below showed that somebody else was looking out of a window. He could not see the face but he knew that it could only be the count. It pleased him that Dracula did not know he was there.

But pleasure immediately turned to fear! With a sudden movement Dracula's whole body came out of the window, and he began to climb head downwards like a fly on the wall, his fingers and toes using every little space between the stones, and his clothes rising up around him like wings. Down he went until he disappeared into the shadows at the bottom of the castle wall.

Almost sick with fright, Jonathan at first could hardly think or act at all. What was this Dracula? He hardly noticed that the cross which he had been wearing round his neck had caught on a piece of iron and fallen out of the window. He had come to think it had some power over Dracula. Now it was gone. He felt weak and lay down on a bed opposite the window waiting for his strength to return.

What happened next was so strange that it could have been a dream. Even with his eyes closed he knew that he was not alone. Three young women were watching him from the shadows, and talking in low voices. As they moved out into the moonlight he saw through half-open eyes that all three were very beautiful, and when they laughed the moonlight shone on long, white teeth.

As they came nearer, Jonathan could see excitement in their reddish eyes, and hear it in their breathing and the way they laughed. They were evil and he feared them, but at the same time something made him share their excitement, and he wanted them to come on.

At last, pushed forward by the other two, the fairest girl knelt down beside the bed and put her face close to his. Jonathan felt her breath on his neck and two sharp teeth just touching and resting lightly on his skin. He closed his eyes and waited, unable and unwilling to move.

What followed was like being in the middle of a storm. Jonathan felt that the count was present even before he

13

The three women

saw his hand fix on the neck of the woman by his bedside and throw her across the room. He had never appeared so angry. His face was as white as death against the fire of his eyes, and his whole body shook.

"How dare you touch him? How dare you disobey my orders?"

"You do not understand. You are not a woman," said one of them, and all three laughed.

"Did I or did I not say that he was not to be touched?"

"Master, he was lying there. What could we do?"

"This man is mine ... until I have no further use for him. And then, only then ..." Dracula left his sentence unfinished, but its meaning for Jonathan was clear.

"So, are we to have nothing tonight?" asked another of the women, looking at the bag at Dracula's feet. It moved, and from it came a cry such as a child might make. He kicked it across to them and they pulled at it like hungry animals, while the cries from inside became louder. Mist entered the room, and a sleep that he could not fight against came over Jonathan. But the secret of Castle Dracula was to him a secret no longer. It was a house of vampires!

Chapter 3
Vampires!

Jonathan woke up in his own bed. Had it been a dream, after all? Why, then, were his clothes arranged in an unusual way, and why was his watch in the wrong place? He dressed and went down to the door leading to the other part of the castle. It was now not only locked: it had been shut with such angry force that some of the wall had fallen out. It had been no dream.

That evening the count said nothing about the night before, but brought out more writing paper and asked Jonathan to write Mina three letters. The first was to say that his work was nearly done and that he would leave in a few days; the second that he was starting the next morning; and the third that he had left the castle and arrived in Bistritz.

"The posts are slow," he said. "I do not want your friends to think that something has happened to you. I will post these letters at the right time so they will know when to expect you."

"What can I do but obey?" Jonathan asked himself. "I'm completely in his power."

The next day began well. He woke to the sound of voices – ordinary men's voices. Running to the dining room window he looked out and saw some gipsies in a corner of the courtyard, unloading long wooden boxes from a cart. The sight of ordinary people, even these wild Transylvanian gipsies, gave hope. Down in the courtyard were free men who could, perhaps, carry a letter to the outside world.

He ran to his room to get the paper that he kept in his bag. But where was his bag with his ticket and his money? Where was the suit he travelled in, and his coat? All gone! What new evil was Dracula planning?

When he returned to the window the gipsies had disappeared. But for the rest of the day Jonathan could hear the sound of digging. Something was going on, and to find out what it was he could only watch the count. That evening he sat down by his bedroom window and waited for the sound of finger and toe taking hold of the wall.

Just after the sun had gone down he heard it. Dracula was already out of the window and moving down just as he had done the night before. But there was a difference – this time he was wearing Jonathan's clothes!

Everything now became clear. He was going to show himself in Bistritz, post the letters and make people believe that Jonathan was already on his way home. Nobody would think he was still in the castle, where anything could happen to him. He had to escape. He had to get the key of the door, and to do that he had to get into the count's room.

This room lay just below his own. With a rope he could climb straight down. But the count did not leave such things about for his visitors. He looked round. His own room had long curtains. He could take down the strong brass bar which they hung from and put the ends against the wall at the sides of his window. The curtain would then hang down over the count's window. The spaces between the stones were wide enough to get his toes into. It would be dangerous, but it had to be done.

There was nothing he could do that night. Night had its dangers in the castle. Besides, the count might have the key with him. "I must wait until tomorrow," he thought.

17

"Count Dracula doesn't appear much in the mornings, so he almost certainly sleeps then. That'll be the time."

As he sat on the edge of the window, holding the curtain, Jonathan wished (not for the first time since he had arrived at Castle Dracula) that he was somewhere else. But everything went well, and he was soon standing in the count's room.

"But is it really the count's room?" he asked himself. It looked as if it had not been used for years. Thick dust covered everything, even a lot of gold coins lying in a corner. Certainly there were no keys. Did these stone stairs lead down to the real bedroom?

As he went down, the strange, earthy smell of Dracula's breath became noticeable. The further Jonathan went, the stronger and more unpleasant it became. It was like a fox-hole. At last he came into a room with an earth floor, lit by a small, high window. At the far end of the room were the boxes that the gipsies had brought – about fifty of them – all of them now filled with earth. Near them was another, older box. The morning sun now coming in through the window fell on it, and as if led by the sun, Jonathan walked across and looked inside. One look was enough. He fell back with a wild cry.

Dracula lay asleep on a bed of earth. His face was no longer pale but deep red, and his hair, instead of its usual black, was now iron-grey. Blood ran from the corners of his mouth, down his neck and on to his clothes. His whole body was swollen with blood. He smelt of blood. And on his face was the look of a wild animal that has killed and fed until it can feed no more.

Jonathan had to force himself to touch this bag of blood that was Dracula's body. But he could not leave now

Dracula asleep in his box

without going through Dracula's pockets to look for the key. He searched, but they were empty. Dracula was too clever to be caught like this.

For the first time in his life Jonathan wanted to kill – to destroy this hateful thing lying in its box. He looked round and saw a heavy stone that had fallen from the wall. He picked it up and lifted it above his head . . . and let it fall to the ground. It was no use trying to kill something that could not be killed. He was sure that vampires did not die like ordinary men.

Back in his room Jonathan threw himself on to his bed in a state of complete hopelessness. There he was, not only the helpless prisoner of a vampire, but worse – he was actively helping that vampire to seek fresh blood in a new country.

That night the count appeared at his usual time, and not red and swollen as he had appeared earlier.

"Tonight, my friend, we must say goodbye. Tomorrow you return to your own country, and I, too, have a journey to make. In the morning my carriage will take you to the Bistritz road, and you will be in Bistritz by tomorrow evening. I hope I shall see you again at Castle Dracula."

"Why can't I go tonight?" asked Jonathan.

"Because, my dear sir, my carriage is busy."

"But I could walk. I want to go now."

"And your bags?"

"I don't care about them. I can send for them later."

The count smiled. "Come! You shall not wait in my house an hour longer than you wish; though I am sad at your going, and sad that you wish to go so quickly." He led the way down the stairs to the great door. "Listen!" he said.

From quite near came the sound of many wolves. It

was as if the sound rose as soon as Dracula had raised his hand. He began to open the door, which was now unlocked. As he opened it the sound of the wolves became louder, and soon Jonathan could see them jumping up and down, their hungry red mouths wide open. The door continued to open little by little, and Jonathan began to see that only the count stood between him and the wolves. Was this what he had planned – to let him be eaten by these animals who came and went like servants, and whom he called his children?

"Shut the door! I shall wait till morning," cried Jonathan at last, turning away so that Dracula should not see the tears he could no longer hold back. The door closed with a crash, and the sound of the wolves died away.

As he walked back up the stairs he turned and saw the count laughing soundlessly.

Half an hour later he heard horses and the songs of the gipsies in the courtyard. He looked down and saw the cart loaded with wooden boxes. Inside one of them Dracula was on his way to England. The next morning Jonathan, too, would be free to leave. He knew there would be no carriage; but he could walk. He did not fear wolves in the daytime with Dracula away.

One difficulty remained. Dracula had gone, and that was good. But it was night, and night's dangers did not go away with Dracula. While present, the count had kept Jonathan safe from these. "Who will guard me now?" Dracula's words to the three women came back to him ". . . until I have no further use for him." That moment had now arrived. He listened. At first everything was very quiet. But then he began to hear laughing, and the sound of silk dresses in corners. His blood ran cold. These women had him in their power. "Will I ever see England and Mina again?" he thought.

Chapter 4
Mina and Lucy

Mina Murray was a pretty girl, but her friend Lucy Westenra was very beautiful. Many men had fallen in love with Lucy; the two she liked best were Jack Seward and his friend Arthur Holmewood. Arthur and she were deeply in love. Jack Seward was the doctor in charge of a hospital for mad people north of London.

The two girls were on holiday together in Whitby when a strange ship arrived in the river. There was no one alive on the ship, but as it struck the river bank a huge black dog suddenly appeared. It jumped off the ship and disappeared in the narrow streets of the old town. Nobody in Whitby knew anything about the ship, except one merchant, who had orders to take certain heavy wooden boxes off it and send them to London.

That night Mina woke up with a strange feeling. Lucy was not in the room. Mina ran out of the house. It was dark, but suddenly the moon came from behind a cloud and she saw her friend half-sitting, half-lying on their favourite seat. A long black shape was bending over her.

Mina cried out and ran towards her friend. Lucy was quite alone, still half-lying with her head over the back of the seat and her neck bare. Back in the house, Mina noticed two little red marks on Lucy's neck.

The next night, Mina locked the bedroom door and took the key to bed with her. She did not want Lucy to walk in her sleep again. Lucy did get up again that night. Twice Mina heard her try to open the door, and later she tried to pull back the curtains.

Mina put her back to bed, and then looked out of the

window herself. The moon was full, and she could see clearly, but there was nothing moving outside the window – except for a large bat. It was flying in circles, coming close to the window.

In the next few days, Lucy ate, slept and had plenty of fresh air, but she grew paler and weaker. Twice Mina found her during the night, lying with her head out of the open window, as if asleep. The little wounds in her neck did not get better; they were still open and growing larger.

A letter came for Mina. It was from the sister in charge of a hospital in Budapest. Jonathan Harker was in the hospital. He was very ill. "When he arrived here," the sister wrote, "he talked wildly about wolves, blood and vampires. We do not know how he came here, but something evil had happened to him."

Mina had been very unhappy because Jonathan had not written to her. Now she understood.

"Oh, Lucy!" she said. "He is safe, but I must go to him."

One of the madmen in Jack Seward's hospital was behaving very strangely. He kept on saying, "The master is near." And then one night he escaped. With surprising strength he bent the bars of his window. Dr Seward and his men caught Renfield, the madman, outside a church near Carfax House. They carried him back to the hospital, kicking and struggling. A bat flying in and out of the trees seemed to excite him more.

Arthur Holmewood came to see Dr Seward and asked him to go and see Lucy. Lucy's mother lived at Hillingdon, not far from Dr Seward's hospital. Lucy had returned to her mother's house when Mina went to Budapest.

"Lucy is so weak," Arthur said, "that she can hardly move about, and she is getting worse every day."

Dr Seward went at once. Lucy was pale and weak, but he could find no reason for her state – except for two rather nasty-looking insect bites on her neck. He sent some blood to London for a check, but the report came back: nothing the matter with it.

But there *was* something the matter with Lucy. It was a most unusual case, and for unusual cases he knew just one man – his old teacher and friend, Professor Van Helsing of Amsterdam.

Renfield bends the bars of his window

Chapter 5
Professor Van Helsing

Professor Abraham Van Helsing arrived in Hillingdon three days later. He stayed long enough to look at Lucy – whom he saw alone – and then went straight back to Amsterdam. He did not say very much after seeing her, but Seward felt he had not wasted the great man's time.

Van Helsing was interested in the case, and asked for daily reports on Lucy's condition to be sent to him.

The next day Lucy seemed better. Van Helsing had been good for her. Young women liked him, and Lucy trusted him. The day after that, Dr Seward was able to send an even better report. It was as if a dark cloud which had been lying over her was lifting.

But if Lucy seemed better, Renfield did not. Since his escape his spirits had been very low. He sat in a corner looking lifeless and saying little. Seward tried to get him to talk sometimes, but all he would say was: "He has left me. There is no hope. He has left me."

On the third day after Van Helsing's visit Lucy was again so ill that Seward sent off a telegram asking him to come at once.

The professor arrived the following evening, and Seward led him up to Lucy's room. He had never seen her look so ill. She was so pale that even her lips and the inside of her mouth seemed to have lost colour. Her breathing was painful to see and hear, and she hardly had the strength to speak. Van Helsing looked at her in silence, then led the way outside. He was about to speak when an excited voice was heard below, and Arthur Holmewood came running up the stairs.

"I came as soon as I could. She is worse, I hear," he said.

"She is in the greatest danger, young man," Van Helsing replied.

"Danger?" cried Arthur. "But what can be done? I would give the last drop of my blood to save her."

"My dear sir, I do not ask as much as that – not the last drop. But blood is exactly what she needs. She has hardly enough blood to keep up the action of her heart. The blood of a young and healthy man like you is what she needs. Please, Mr Holmewood – for I suppose you are Mr Holmewood – take your coat off at once. Dr Seward, we must do this direct."

Without a word, Arthur pulled off his coat and began to roll up the arm of his shirt. Poor Lucy was too ill to feel the opening that the two doctors made in her arm. But ten minutes later the flow of blood from Arthur's arm began to give colour again to her pale face, and her breathing became easier.

"We shall now leave Miss Lucy to sleep. Tomorrow I shall return to see how she is. But we have one more thing to do before we leave."

He went downstairs and returned with a box which he laid on Lucy's bed. "Go on, open it," he said with a smile. Lucy put her hand in the box and pulled out some little white flowers.

"For me? Oh, Dr Van Helsing, how kind!" she said.

"Yes, my dear, for you," replied the professor. "But they are for your illness and not for your pleasure. Smell them."

Lucy put the flowers to her nose.

"Oh!" she said. "Why, these are garlic flowers! They

Dr Seward with Lucy

are just common garlic. Is it a joke, Professor?"

To Seward's surprise Van Helsing did not laugh. Indeed, he looked more serious than he had ever seen him look before. He laid his hand on Lucy's and said: "This is no joke. There is a reason for everything that I do. I warn you to obey me in everything, or you will find yourself in danger of death – yes, and worse!"

Then, seeing that he had frightened her, he continued in a gentler voice: "Do not be afraid. I am only trying to help you. There is great power in these very ordinary flowers."

What the professor did next was not to be found in any book that Seward had ever read. First he shut all the windows. Then, taking a handful of the flowers, he rubbed them all round the windows, the door and the fireplace.

"Well, Professor," said Seward, "I know you always have a reason for everything you do, but I am glad there is no other doctor here to see what you are doing. He would say that you had stopped being a doctor and become a magician. It's as if you were trying to keep out an evil spirit."

"Perhaps I am," Van Helsing answered quietly, as he began to make the rest of the flowers into a ring. When he had done so he put it round Lucy's neck and said:

"Whatever you do tonight, do not open the windows or the door. And do not take away the flowers from your neck. It is a matter of life or death!"

The next day Van Helsing arrived at the hospital at eight o'clock to collect Dr Seward. They went on together to the Westenra house, where they were met by Mrs Westenra.

"I hope you will find Lucy better," she said. "I've just looked into her room, but she was sleeping well, so I did not wake her up."

"So my treatment is working," said the professor, looking pleased.

"Perhaps it was my treatment," replied Mrs Westenra with a smile. "I went into her room before I went to bed last night and found her sleeping quietly. But there was no air in the room. And there was such a strong smell from some flowers round her neck that I thought they would be bad for the poor child in her weak condition. I took them away and opened the window a little. You will be pleased with her, I am sure."

Van Helsing turned deadly pale. He said nothing, but Seward could see that he was trying not to show his feelings. He knew very well the danger of giving a shock to Mrs Westenra. But as soon as she left the room they ran up the stairs to Lucy. While Seward pulled open the curtains, Van Helsing bent over the still sleeping Lucy.

"It is as I feared," he said, staring at Lucy's pale face. "At least she has not lost as much this time . . . Jack, I must return to Amsterdam today, but you must sleep in this house every night. Boxes of fresh flowers will arrive every day, and you must do exactly what I did last night. I shall return in four days, or before, if needed. Guard her well."

"Guard her?" asked Seward. "Against what? – or whom?" He felt a moment of uncertainty and fear.

"Whom! That is better, Jack. You were always a quick student. But you have more to learn yet." And Van Helsing was gone.

Chapter 6
The fight for Lucy's life

The next few days were hard for Jack Seward. It was the hospital by day, and Hillingdon by night. It would have been easier if he had known what he was guarding Lucy against, but Van Helsing had said no more.

Every morning a fresh box of garlic flowers arrived by special post from Holland, and Seward did exactly as the professor had shown him the first night. He did not like it, because it seemed to him unscientific, and Dr Seward was a very scientific doctor. But it seemed to work. From day to day the colour came back into Lucy's face, and even the little wounds in her neck were beginning to close.

But the nights were tiring. Several times he was woken up by strange sounds which seemed to come from outside Lucy's window. At first he thought it was the branch of a tree which was brushing against the window in the wind. But the next day he could see that there was no tree there. Some nights it was like the sound of wings.

Renfield had also caused trouble. One day Dr Hennessey, Seward's helper, reported that Renfield had suddenly attacked two men. He had been walking in the garden with his keeper when he noticed these men driving a cart along the road from Carfax. The keeper had only just been able to pull Renfield away. Dr Hennessey had thought it wise to give some money to the men, and to take their names in case there was trouble later.

Early one evening Seward was sitting in his office taking a quiet look at the evening newspaper before going over to Hillingdon as usual. Tired from writing reports, he was almost falling asleep over a story about a wolf that had just escaped from the London Zoo. He was half dreaming about the wolf bursting into his room when the door opened, and in burst – not a wolf – but Renfield, looking quite as wild as a wolf, with something shining in his hand.

"Oh my God!" Seward cried. It was a kitchen knife.

He tried to keep the table between them, but Renfield was too quick, and struck his left arm – before being knocked down with a heavy stone paper-weight held in the doctor's right hand.

Renfield lay face down on the floor. The knife had fallen from his hand, and the moment of danger had passed. As Seward stood there in a state of shock, holding his wounded arm, he could hear his men running along the passage. He felt bad. Blood from his wound was dripping on to the floor where Renfield lay. And as the guards entered the room, Renfield raised his head and showed a bloody mouth. He had been drinking the doctor's blood as it fell to the floor!

"The blood is the life," he screamed as they led him away. A feeling of sickness came over Seward. Hands reached out to hold him up and he remembered nothing more.

Seward sat up in bed feeling very weak. Perhaps he had lost more blood than he thought. Looking at his watch, he saw it was ten o'clock – time he was at Hillingdon. But was he well enough to go? Dr Hennessey walked in: "Hillingdon? Impossible, my dear Seward. It is my clear duty as a doctor to tell you to stay in bed."

In the end it was arranged that Dr Hennessey should himself drive over to Hillingdon and look in at the Westenra house before he went to bed. Somebody ought to spend the night there, but Seward did not want Hennessey to know too much about Lucy's case. The professor had made it quite clear: what happened at Hillingdon must be kept quite secret. Besides, Seward did not want other doctors to know about this "magic" with the garlic flowers, so he only asked Dr Hennessey to tell Lucy to "make the usual arrangements". She would understand.

Because his arm hurt, Seward did not sleep well that night. And when he did get to sleep at last his rest was cut short by the arrival of an early telegram. The boy who brought it said it ought to have arrived the evening before, but it had been sent to another village of the same name by mistake. The telegram read:

Do not fail to be at Hillingdon tonight. Very important. Will arrive early on 19th. Van Helsing.

"Good Heavens!" cried Seward. "That was last night. What can Van Helsing mean?"

He did not wait for breakfast, but drove straight over to Hillingdon. It was still early, and he did not want to wake Lucy or her mother, so he rang quietly, hoping to bring a servant to the door. No answer. He rang again. Still no answer. He put his ear to the letter box. Everything was as quiet as a tomb. He felt that something was wrong.

He walked round the house looking for an open window, but Van Helsing's orders had been obeyed; everything was carefully shut and locked – until he came to Mrs Westenra's room, which was on the ground floor in order to save her from climbing the stairs. There he found the window broken and blood on the glass. And in the flower-bed below the window there were marks of an animal's feet. They could have been made by a dog or – if the idea did not seem so foolish – by a wolf. Seward looked round him. The house and garden were unnaturally quiet. He bent down to look at the marks more closely, and almost at once heard a sound on the path behind him. He sprang up ready to defend himself, but it was only Van Helsing. In a few breathless words he told the professor about Renfield and the telegram.

"I am afraid we are too late," Van Helsing said, putting his hand through the broken window. He opened it, and one after the other they climbed in.

On the bed lay Lucy and her mother. On Mrs Westenra's face was a look of fear such as Seward had never seen before. He felt her hand. She was quite dead. In her other hand was a tightly held ring of flowers. In a moment of fear she must have reached out for her daughter and pulled the flowers from her neck.

Lucy lay by her side. The wounds in her neck, which before had been closing up, were now wide open, and had an eaten look. Van Helsing held her hand and placed his ear close to her chest. The seconds passed like hours.

"It is not too late," he cried at last. "Quick. Get some whisky!"

Seward ran into the dining room. It was not surprising that the maids had not answered the door. They were lying on the floor. He bent down to smell their breath. Something had been put in their drink to make them sleep. He picked up a bottle and returned to the bedroom, where Van Helsing rubbed the liquid over Lucy's hands, arms and face. Seward then told the professor about the maids.

"Go and wake them," said Van Helsing. "We need hot water. She must be kept warm. And send for Mr Holmewood. We may not be able to save her, and he must be prepared for the worst."

Because she was so weak, Van Helsing thought it was unwise to try to give her fresh blood, so he let her sleep on. Seward sat watching her. It was strange how her thinness made her teeth appear longer and sharper than usual. But when she opened her eyes at last, she looked the lovely young girl he knew and loved.

Arthur was brave. He sat with Lucy all the time, his face never showing the sadness in his heart. Van Helsing later came in and sent him off to try to sleep in the sitting room while Seward remained with Lucy.

About six o'clock in the morning Van Helsing came in to give him a rest. He undid the silk handkerchief that he had tied round her neck.

"Look!" he cried. Seward looked, and a strange, cold feeling passed over him. The wounds on her neck had completely disappeared.

"She is now dying," said Van Helsing sadly. "It will not be long now. Wake that young man so that he can be with her at the end."

With his usual thoughtfulness Van Helsing had brushed her hair so that it lay all around her head in golden waves. When Arthur came she opened her eyes. "Arthur, my love," she said in a low voice.

Arthur bent down to kiss her but Van Helsing, who had been watching closely, stopped him. "No, not yet. Just hold her hand." Lucy's eyes closed and she seemed to sleep. Seward noticed again the strange changes that he had seen during the night: the tight skin, the open mouth and the long, sharp teeth.

Then in a soft, sleepy voice Lucy spoke again: "Arthur, kiss me." As Arthur bent down she opened her eyes, and Seward was shocked to see how hard and stone-like they had become. Van Helsing had also noticed something, and before Arthur could kiss her he pulled him back with all his strength.

"Not for your life – not for your living soul!" he said.

Seward, keeping his eyes on Lucy, saw an angry shadow pass across her face, and her sharp teeth closed. A moment later she was the pale, tired, dying girl. She tried to smile but had not the strength. It was as if two Lucys were living in the same body.

Van Helsing softened. "Come, my boy. Take her hand in yours and kiss her now. But not on the lips, and only once." Arthur did so, and Lucy's eyes closed. Her breathing became more difficult, until at last it stopped.

"It is all over," said Seward in a dead voice.

"No," Van Helsing replied. "I wish it was. But it is only just beginning!"

Chapter 7
Lucy is a vampire!

After death, Lucy looked so unnaturally beautiful that it was frightening.

The next morning, a letter addressed to her arrived. Arthur had come for the funeral and he knew the handwriting, Mina's. They opened it. It told them only that Jonathan and Mina had got married in Budapest and had then returned to Exeter.

"Ask her to come to London," Van Helsing said. "She may be able to tell me things that I need to know." And although he was a busy man, he asked if he could stay with Dr Seward. He hoped to see Mina, but Seward felt that this was not his only reason for staying.

A few days after the funeral, the newspapers began to report attacks on young children in north London. The children disappeared, but they were found later – after midnight – looking weak and pale, and with neck wounds.

Van Helsing read the reports. "What do you think?" he asked.

Seward was surprised. "These things are a little like the case of Lucy," he said.

"Only a little like? Have you still no idea how Lucy died? She had lost too much blood. How? Through wounds in her neck, like these children. Now tell me: what made those wounds?"

"I have heard of vampire bats in South America which take blood in this way, but we do not have such bats here in England. – You want me to say that a vampire – a man vampire – made these wounds. Only a madman would believe such things."

Van Helsing was sorry for the young doctor. "There is something worse that I must say. The vampire that drank these children's blood was not the same as the vampire that drank Lucy's. The vampire that attacked the children was Lucy herself!"

Jack Seward was very angry. But Van Helsing knew that first there was one vampire, and now there were two. Next week, next month there might be three, four or five. He had to stop this. But he needed help.

"It is the truth," Van Helsing said, "and of course it is hard for you to believe it or to bear it. But I can prove it if you will come with me."

He took Seward first to the hospital to see one of the children. They looked at the marks on the child's neck – just like the marks on Lucy's neck. Then the two doctors went to the family tomb where Lucy's coffin lay.

"What are you going to do?" Jack asked.

Van Helsing undid the top of the coffin. Then he began to cut the lead which had surrounded the body inside the coffin.

There was nothing in the coffin.

"Now we must wait outside the tomb," Van Helsing said.

It was a long wait. Long after midnight, they saw a white shape moving among the trees towards the tomb. Van Helsing stepped forward. The shape seemed to see him, and disappeared, leaving on the ground a small child, still asleep.

As daylight showed in the east, the two doctors returned to the tomb. The coffin was no longer empty. Lucy lay there, not like a body some time dead, but more beautiful than ever.

Van Helsing pulled back the lips and showed the teeth.

"See, they are like knife points. How many more times must they sink into a child's neck before you believe?"

Seward's eyes were fixed on the evil beauty of the face.

"What must we do?" he asked.

"Cut off her head, fill the mouth with garlic, and drive a thick piece of wood through her heart. But not now. We are not prepared. And we shall need more help. Arthur Holmewood must join us."

Chapter 8
Lucy's soul is saved

It had been difficult to get Arthur to the tomb, but he had come – thanks to Jack Seward. Van Helsing knew that Seward's words would have more effect than his own. But he also knew that neither his words nor Seward's could make Arthur believe that Lucy was a vampire. Only Lucy herself could do that.

Some time after midnight the three men – Van Helsing holding a long bag – stood round the coffin.

"Dr Seward," Van Helsing said, "when we left this tomb early this morning, was the body of Miss Lucy in her coffin or was it not?"

"It was, Professor."

"I will now," said he in the manner of a magician, "open the coffin." He opened it. The coffin was empty.

There was a long silence. Then Arthur said in a low voice: "Professor, I know that you would not remove her body. Who would – who *could* do such a thing?"

Van Helsing did not answer, but led the way out of the tomb. He locked the door, and then from his bag took some bread wrapped up in a white cloth. He rolled it between his hands and pressed it into the space between the door and the surrounding stone of the tomb, and into the keyhole.

"This is bread which has been blessed in church," he said. "I am closing the tomb so that nothing evil may enter."

"And now?" asked Arthur, still shocked by the disappearance of Lucy's body.

"Now," said Van Helsing, "prepare yourselves. You

will need great strength of mind. Let us wait behind this tree from where we can see the tomb."

He spoke as if he knew exactly what was going to happen, but even he felt doubt and fear. He was being drawn deeper and deeper into the unnatural world of the Un-Dead, as vampires were called. As he looked round he thought he had never seen a place at night which promised so much evil. The tombstones shone white like the bones of the dead, and every time the wind blew he seemed to hear the movement of wings and of things in the grass. He knew that he could not have stayed there alone.

No one spoke. Even the wind dropped at last, leaving a deep dream-like silence. An hour passed, and then a sound! Jack Seward was drawing in his breath. He pointed. Some distance away between two long lines of trees a white figure had appeared, holding something in its arms.

It stopped in a little pool of moonlight, and this time it was all too clear. A golden-haired woman dressed in a white funeral cloth was coming forward holding a small child. She came on until she was quite close enough for all of them to see. It was Lucy – but a Lucy quite changed, her lips wet with the fresh blood of the child. It ran down her face and coloured the white cloth that she was clothed in.

Van Helsing stepped out. She drew back with an angry noise, throwing to the ground the child, which up to then she had been guarding as a dog guards a bone. The child's sharp cry drew an answering cry from Arthur, and immediately Lucy changed again. She had noticed Arthur, and stretched out a hand to him in a way that was so natural, so like the old Lucy. "Arthur," she said, "leave your friends and come with me."

There was something so sweet in her voice that even

Van Helsing felt drawn. As for Arthur he stood as if held by magic. She smiled again, and he walked towards her. But Van Helsing was ready. Before Lucy could fix her teeth in Arthur's neck he sprang forward holding in front of him his little gold cross. With a wild cry, as if she had been touched by a red-hot iron, Lucy jumped back, then ran to the door of the tomb. But there again she stopped. Van Helsing had done his work well. At last she ran into the shadow of a tree. All that they could see of her was the white of her teeth shining in the darkness.

There was silence. Both the living and the Un-Dead were in a state of shock. At last Van Helsing, still holding up his cross, turned to Arthur and in a shaking voice asked: "Am I to go further in my work?"

Arthur went down on his knees and hid his face in his hands. "Do what you think must be done. There can be nothing worse than what I have already seen."

The professor walked back to the door of the tomb and picked out some of the bread. As if pulled by some power she could not stand against, Lucy moved from the shadows back to the tomb and disappeared through the narrow space that he had opened. He then put the bread back.

"My friends, there is nothing more that we can do before daylight. She cannot come out. She is tired, and perhaps weak, having not fed properly for two nights. She will soon sleep. And then——" he said, "we will do our work."

As the three men waited for sunrise the wildest thoughts ran through their minds. The sky reddened and the sun rose. Seward and Arthur waited for a word from the professor, but he seemed in no hurry to begin. At last he pulled out a heavy gold watch.

45

"It is half-past six," he said. "We have half an hour."

Lucy was asleep, and as beautiful as she had ever been. Arthur, so pale that he might have been dead himself, wept openly as he bent over the coffin. But Van Helsing did not feel as Arthur felt. He could only see the dried blood on her mouth. He opened his bag and took out some doctor's knives, a thick, round, pointed piece of wood about a metre long and a heavy hammer.

"Vampires cannot die through age," he said, "but live on, feeding on blood, and turning others into vampires like themselves. So the circle of the Un-Dead widens all the time.

"Those little children whose blood she has drunk will not suffer. But those who give their blood too often learn to love the vampire and become vampires themselves after they die. For you, my friend Arthur, it would have been most dangerous to give yourself to her.

"But there is a way to set the souls of the Un-Dead free – free from a life of evil and an after-life of endless punishment." He pointed to the hammer. "I think it would be a blessed thing to do – to strike and save a soul. I could do this. But would it not be better for the one she loved best to do it?"

"Oh my true friend," said Arthur, "tell me what to do, and I shall not fail."

"Brave man," said Van Helsing. "Take this piece of wood in one hand and place the point over her heart. Then, when I have read the prayer for the dead from this prayer book here – strike in God's name!"

Still pale, but with a strong hand, Arthur took the piece of wood and the hammer. Van Helsing began to read, while Dr Seward placed the point directly over the heart. The prayer ended, and Arthur struck with all his strength.

Lucy in her coffin with blood on her mouth

The body in the coffin jumped as if it had received an electric shock, and the mouth opened to let out a cry that made their hair stand up like brushes. The whole body turned this way and that, and the sharp teeth opened and shut until the lips were red with their own blood. But Arthur did not stop. His right arm rose and fell again and again as he drove the point further and further in, until at last the wild movement of the body stopped. It was all over.

"Before you leave this tomb," said Van Helsing, "look for the last time on Lucy's face. She is not now one of the Un-Dead."

Arthur looked, and it was true. After all the blood and pain Lucy was at peace. She was not a vampire, she was the Lucy he had loved and saved at last. He kissed her for the last time and walked out into the sunlight.

The two doctors cut the top off the piece of wood, leaving the point in the body, filled the mouth with garlic, cut off her head and then closed the coffin lid. The professor locked the door and gave the key to Arthur.

"The first part of our work is done," he said, "but the greater part remains: to find and destroy the cause of Lucy's sorrow. All I want to know is this: are you ready to follow me into further danger?"

"Where you go, I will follow," said Jack Seward. "It's our duty to destroy this evil."

They looked at Arthur, but they did not have to ask. He had the look of a man who only wanted one thing from life, and would not rest until he had found it.

Chapter 9
Dracula's house

So Van Helsing had gathered his little army. But where was the enemy? In the case of Lucy the battle-lines were clear. But Van Helsing could not wait for the enemy to show himself. He was not a man who liked waiting. Besides, there was another path to follow.

It was this path that led him to Paddington Station the following day, where he waited for the arrival of Jonathan and Mina Harker.

Since his return from Transylvania, Jonathan had been living quietly. He had suffered a bad shock, and Mina had kept him away from London. Now he was better, and she had decided to go to London to see Van Helsing as he had often asked her to.

The train arrived, and the three of them went back to Van Helsing's hotel. First Mina told the story of her stay in Whitby. He liked this young woman who knew what to do at difficult moments. And then Jonathan told his story, and Van Helsing could hardly hold back his excitement. "But why," he asked, "have you not told this to anybody before?"

"Oh Professor," said Mina, "it was weeks before he was well enough to tell the story even to me. And who but me would have believed it?"

Van Helsing then told them all that had happened since Lucy's death. "You will believe my story," he said, "as I believe yours. But, as you say, who else would believe? That is why this evil can only be fought by us. I want you to join us. We meet tonight at Dr Seward's. You, Mr Harker, know better than any of us the dangers I am asking you to face."

Mina looked at Jonathan's pale, lined face and his greying hair. She hated the evil power that had made the man she loved look so old before his time.

"I will help you," she said.

"If Mina helps you, I will, too," said Jonathan at last. From the way he said it Van Helsing understood that he had not decided lightly.

"We shall expect you at seven," said Van Helsing. "From what you have told me I see we have no time to lose. Indeed, we may already be too late."

". . . so, my friends. These are the facts we have discovered about our enemy. As we have seen, he is powerful, but he has weaknesses. Above all, he needs a place of rest during the hours of daylight. If we can catch him in his box we can destroy him."

"*If*," said Seward. "But we need to know where these boxes are."

"And thanks to Jonathan," replied Van Helsing, "we do know. They lie only a hundred metres or so from the room where we are now – in Carfax House!"

"In Carfax House!" Jack Seward and Arthur Holmewood almost spoke the words together. Van Helsing liked to surprise, and his words had all the result he wanted.

"Carfax is Dracula's house," said Jonathan. "They must be there."

"That explains the case of Renfield," said Seward. "It must have been this Dracula that so excited him. Why, a week or two ago he escaped and led us into the grounds of Carfax . . . to the doors of the old church . . . the boxes must be there!"

"What are we waiting for?" cried Arthur. "Let's go!"

"Not so fast." Van Helsing did not like hurry. "We must first prepare ourselves." He took from his pocket a little gold cross and hung it round the neck of Jonathan, who was nearest to him, together with a circle of garlic flowers which he took from a box. He did the same to Seward and Arthur. But when he came to Mina he said:

"Madam Mina, I will not ask you to join us. It will not be woman's work. You have already travelled far today and will wish to rest."

Mina said she was not tired. She wanted to go with them. But Van Helsing would not allow her to, and the four men went off by themselves into the night.

Jack Seward had brought with him a lot of old keys on a ring. He tried fourteen before the fifteenth turned. The door opened inwards without a push. It was as if they were expected.

Making a cross in the air with his right hand, Van Helsing was the first to enter. The floor was thick with dust, and they could see the many marks of boots. Someone had been in not long ago. But what they noticed most was the smell.

"It is his breath," said Jonathan. "How well I remember it."

They saw at once what they had come for. The earth boxes lay one on top of the other against the walls. But how many were there? A hurried count showed that out of fifty only twenty-nine remained!

Van Helsing swore quietly. The enemy was still ahead. He started to recount the boxes " . . . twenty-two, twenty-three——" He stopped. Arthur was pulling at his arm.

"Have you noticed," he said, "that it seems to be getting

51

less dark." They all stopped counting and looked around them. Every corner of the building was filling up with points of reddish fire. Then little movements, little noises started. For a time they all stood and stared. And then they understood. The church was filling with hundreds – no, thousands of rats!

They ran for the door and the rats ran for them. There were rats under their feet; rats running over their feet; rats climbing up their trousers; rats in their hair. Long fat rats hung on to their clothes by their teeth. They shook them off, but more and more came on, their eyes burning up the darkness.

Somehow they all reached the door. Outside it was safe, but it was some time before any of them could speak.

"When we come back tomorrow," said Van Helsing at last, "Arthur had better bring his dogs."

"Tomorrow!" cried Seward. "I don't want to come back here ever again."

"We shall have to, whether we like it or not," was the reply. "The boxes must be destroyed." But he was not really thinking of the boxes they were going to destroy. What troubled him was the boxes that were not there. Twenty-one boxes had left Carfax and they had to be found.

Chapter 10
Dracula attacks Mina

"Twenty-one boxes gone, and they might be anywhere," said Van Helsing. The four men were sitting round the table having breakfast.

"Twenty-one boxes make a big load," said Arthur. "If they were taken out by day someone in the hospital might have noticed them. After all, Carfax is very near, and it must have happened in the past three weeks."

Dr Seward put his tea cup down with a crash and hurried out of the room. He reappeared a minute later waving a piece of paper at his surprised friends.

"I should have thought of it before," he cried. "Dr Hennessey's report!" He told them the story of Renfield's attack on the carters; and how Dr Hennessey, fearing some trouble with the law, had taken down their names. "Here they are," he said. "Thomas Snelling and Joseph Smollet. Renfield must have known they were taking Dracula away in one of the boxes."

Dr Seward's news made Van Helsing feel much better, and he began to make plans again. Jonathan went off to London to find the carters, and to find out where they had taken the boxes. The other three returned to Carfax.

By daylight the place was not so frightening, and the dogs that Arthur brought with him to keep off the rats were not needed. There were no rats. Nor was there a body in any of the boxes, so the professor simply opened every box and placed inside it a piece of blessed bread. No vampire could ever rest there again.

Mina, looking rather pale and unwell, was having breakfast when the men returned. Later she went with Dr

Seward round the hospital. She was interested in what he had to say about Renfield and went with the doctor into his room. Renfield was quiet and even friendly that day. He seemed to like Mina, and she asked if she could stay and talk to him.

That afternoon Dr Seward worked, the professor read a book in the garden and Arthur took his dogs for a walk. Later, a telegram arrived from Jonathan saying that he had not finished his search and had decided to spend the night in London. The others passed a pleasant evening together, and one by one they went to bed. This peaceful day did not prepare them for the night that lay ahead.

At twenty minutes past twelve Van Helsing was woken by a frightful cry. As he put on some clothes he heard someone running along the passage to Dr Seward's room. It was the night guard. Renfield had been hurt.

When the doctors reached Renfield's room they found him lying on the floor. He had been struck on the head so hard that the bone had been pushed in. He was alive, but breathing with difficulty.

"Get your bag," said Van Helsing. "We must take away the pressure of this broken bone. We must cut it out at once, or he will die."

"He will die, anyway," replied Seward. "He has been struck with great force. This is not a simple fall."

"If he can at least tell us what happened it may help us," Van Helsing replied as he shaved the bloody hair away from the place where he was going to cut.

The doctors' work had results at once. Renfield's eyes opened, and his lips began to move: "He came," he said.

"Go on," said Seward.

"– through the window in the mist – like the night

54

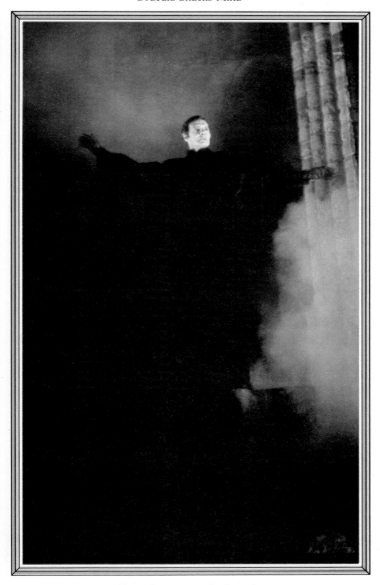

Dracula appears in the mist

before. I knew he wanted blood. Mrs Harker was good to me – I tried to stop him. He threw me down." Poor Renfield's voice became more difficult to hear, and at last he was silent. Dr Seward took his hand. He was dead.

Neither doctor said a word. They ran upstairs, meeting Arthur on the way, and went straight to Mina's room. There they stopped and listened at the door. Everything seemed quiet inside. Was it wise to trust the dying words of a madman?

"This is a matter of life or death," said Van Helsing, as he very gently tried the door. It was locked! At once Arthur threw himself at it with such force that it burst open, throwing the professor on to the floor. He rose to his knees, but the sight that met his eyes so froze his blood that for a moment he could not bring himself to stand.

Dracula stood with his back against the far wall holding Mina close to him. His right arm held her head against his chest. At first sight they appeared like lovers. But Van Helsing saw the open wound in the vampire's neck and the thin stream of blood that flowed down over his chest. He was forcing Mina's face down upon his chest – forcing her to drink his blood, as one might make a young cat drink milk!

It was lucky that Dracula was as surprised as they were. His eyes were circles of fire and his mouth hung open. He threw Mina, her face and night-clothes red with blood, on to the bed and prepared to spring.

But by now Van Helsing was on his feet, holding out his cross towards Dracula. Seward and Arthur did the same. The vampire screamed, and a mist rolled into the room. When it disappeared a few moments later the count was gone.

It was an hour before Mina was able to speak; the shock had been so great.

"It was like a dream," she said. "Like a dream I had the night before. I was just about to go to sleep when a bright-eyed man appeared by my side. He put his hands on me and all my strength flowed away. And then ..." she seemed to have trouble in going on. "Then he opened his shirt, and with his own fingers tore open his neck and made me drink his blood. While I drank – I couldn't help it – while I drank, he said ..."

"Try to go on, my dear," Van Helsing said.

"He said: 'Now we are of one blood and one mind. You have helped my enemies, but soon you will help me.'"

Nobody spoke. What could they say to help?

"But is it true, Professor?" she continued, with tears in her eyes, taking hold of his hand. "Am I tied to Dracula for ever? When I die, must I become ... one of these?"

"My child," replied Van Helsing, looking older and greyer than before. "You are with friends who will give their lives to keep you safe. We have been careless, but we shall not be careless again. If Dracula thinks he has won something by this, he is wrong. We had reason enough to destroy him before. That reason now is a thousand times stronger."

Dracula holds Mina

Chapter 11
The end of Dracula

When Jonathan returned, the news about Mina struck him like a blow, but he had found out where the boxes had gone. He had an address in London.

"We must go there quickly," Van Helsing said. "But we must find a way of guarding Mina."

"I'm coming with you," she said. "you will see that I shall not be afraid."

At the London address they found all but one of Dracula's boxes. They destroyed them, but they did not find the count himself, although it was day.

That night they guarded Mina with great care. In the morning Dr Seward asked her how she felt.

"A little tired," she said. "I was dreaming so much. In my dreams I was always on a boat, and I could hear water."

"Professor," Jack said, "can it be that because of his attack Mina enters Dracula's mind while she is asleep?"

"Yes," said Van Helsing. "And that must mean that Dracula is leaving the country by sea with his last box – going home. We must find out which ship it is on."

"Why?" Mina asked. "Isn't it enough that he is leaving the country?"

Van Helsing took her hands. "Madam Mina, a week ago it would have been enough, but now we have a soul to save."

It was easy to find out the ship. One ship had sailed that week from London for the Black Sea. The *Czarina Catherine* had sailed for Varna that morning, and the ship's office said that at the last moment a man had paid a lot of money to put a box on the ship.

It was an unhappy Jonathan who got off the train at Varna. He knew that the professor and Dr Seward watched Mina all the time for changes – in her teeth, her eyes and her skin. Vampire's blood worked slowly, but surely. Only the death of the vampire whose blood she had tasted could save her.

Their plans were all made, but when the ship should have arrived at Varna, there was a thick – and most unusual – mist. No one saw the *Czarina Catherine* enter the Danube and sail up it to Galatz, three hundred kilometres nearer to Castle Dracula than Varna.

At Galatz they found that a man had collected the box from the ship, and they had to make new plans.

"This is what I think we should do," Van Helsing said. "Dracula will perhaps use the river. Arthur and Jonathan will take a steamboat and go up the river. Jack, I want you to take horses and follow the river bank. Mina and I will take a train to Veresti and from there we will go on towards the castle. If you meet Dracula on the way, deal with him. If you do not find him, we shall be waiting for you in the mountains. It will be our last chance."

When Jonathan had first come to Transylvania, bright sunny days made travelling a joy. Now it was autumn. Early mornings on the river were cold and dark; there were often mists. It was good to feel the warmth as he opened the fire-box of the little steamboat to put on more wood.

In two days sailing, day and night, they passed only a few boats, and these were too small to have a box on board. But on the third day, as they passed into the Bistritza, they heard from some passing Slovaks that a big boat going unusually fast had passed them the day before. This gave them hope.

As they hurried on, the river became narrow and rocky. In the end the boat was damaged, and mending it cost them several hours. The weather was also getting worse.

They were now only about sixty kilometres from Bistritz, and Arthur was afraid that the box had already left the river. So at the next small town they left the boat and took horses. They decided to ride by small country roads towards their meeting place with Mina and the professor. They had not seen Jack Seward since the first day out of Galatz. He could only be on the road ahead.

The professor and Mina arrived at Veresti at midday on the 31st. The train went no further, and the professor went off to find a carriage to take them a hundred kilometres from Veresti to where the Bistritz road went over the mountains. He also bought food and warmer clothes.

"We may not see a town again for a week," he said.

The roads were bad, but Van Helsing was tireless. With only the shortest stops for sleep they drove on and on, changing horses whenever they could. They reached the Bistritz road on the second day.

Mina had been sleeping a lot, but she had stopped dreaming of water. Dracula must have left the river. Now, as they climbed higher into the mountains, Mina seemed to throw off her sleepiness and took great interest in the road. "This is the way," she said at last, pointing to a side road.

"Are you sure?" asked Van Helsing.

"Of course," she replied. "Hasn't my Jonathan travelled this way and told me?"

Van Helsing thought it strange, but he obeyed, and two hours later Mina was proved right. Through a break in the trees they saw for the first time the cloud-wrapped walls of Castle Dracula!

They drew off the road among the trees. Van Helsing saw that it was going to snow. He made a fire. Next, he took a stick, and round the fire and Mina he drew a circle into which he dropped small pieces of blessed bread. He then walked outside the circle and stood looking at Mina sitting by the fire, as silent as the dead.

"Mina," he called, "come here."

She rose and began to walk towards him, then stopped. She seemed unable to take another step. Van Helsing stretched out his hand. "Come," he said.

She shook her head and sank to the ground. It was as he thought. She was already half vampire and could not break out of the circle. But if she could not break out, others could not break in, and he would be safe inside – if it was safe to be with Mina herself. He looked at her. She had gone back to the fire, and was sitting there deep in secret thought.

Darkness fell. Sometimes the horses made frightened noises and pulled at the tree they were tied to. Then Van Helsing went to them and put his hands on them to quieten them. Although he was tired he did not dare to sleep before Mina slept – and she was so wakeful.

About three o'clock in the morning the fire began to die down, and he was just starting off to fetch wood before the snow got worse when Mina spoke: "Don't go out of the circle now. Stay where you are safe."

He stopped. "*I* may be safe, but *you*——"

Mina laughed a low, unnatural laugh: "Do not fear for me. There is no one safer than I am from them."

He was going to ask her who she meant by "them",

when the horses screamed again. He looked and saw three women moving round the edge of the circle like dancers! Fear seized him. They could only be the women of the castle who had drunk Jonathan's blood! They stretched out their arms to Mina as if they were calling her to join them. He could feel Mina's growing excitement. Would the power of the circle hold?

He could not take the chance. Picking up a piece of burning wood, he threw it at them. "In God's name, go!" he cried. And screaming and swearing they went.

Silence returned. He felt more tired than he had ever felt before. But Mina was looking at him in a strange way, and he had to face the frightful truth. It was not safe to sleep in her company. She had almost passed into the world of the Un-Dead.

Day came slowly. It stopped snowing, but the skies remained heavy. On the roads fresh wheelmarks in the light covering of snow showed the three horsemen (Jonathan and Arthur had met Jack Seward the day before on the road) that they were only a little way behind their enemy.

By the early afternoon the gipsies to whom the Slovaks had passed on the box could be seen on the mountain road above them. As the afternoon drew on, and the sun sank slowly in the sky, it became clear to all that it was a race against time.

Suddenly a shot rang out. It was very near. Pulling out his Indian knife, Jonathan kicked his tired horse forward. The last battle was about to begin.

The gipsies had stopped and were gathered round their cart with knives in their hands. Van Helsing stood in the middle of the road in front of them, holding a gun. They seemed undecided what to do. He was one and they were many. He had a gun, but if they all attacked at once ...

They were not given time to decide. The next moment three horsemen were riding straight at them, Jonathan in front, waving his knife and making wild cries.

The gipsies were tired and surprised. They put up a show of fighting but soon ran off down the mountainside.

The sun was already half sunk below the mountain. In minutes Dracula's power would return. Yet the one thing they had forgotten was something with which they could open the box. Picking up stones, they climbed on to the cart and beat the top of the box like madmen. The sun was three-quarters down, and they could feel the body inside begin to move. The wood was breaking up under the force of their stones, and Dracula's face began to appear. The mouth opened, and a low sound came out. The power of evil was waking! Were they too late?

The sun had already gone down when the professor placed the point of a piece of wood he had cut from a tree that day over the vampire's heart. He lifted a huge piece of wood and brought it down hard. To the end of their lives they were to remember Dracula's last scream as his eyes opened and the point went in. It brought Mina running from the trees where she had been hiding. And all five of them gathered round the body of their enemy.

The wild movements of the arms and legs stopped at last, and before their eyes the face, still full of hate, turned from white to yellow to grey. The whole body seemed to go dry and to get smaller. After five minutes it was like some old vegetable. And then it seemed to fall away completely. They watched, unable to pull their eyes away. In ten minutes from the time the point entered Dracula's heart, the whole body had turned to dust, and the evil power that lived in it was no more.

The men turned to Mina. The light was going, but they could see the change. The long teeth, the unnatural colour of the skin, the strange look in her eye had gone. She was again the Mina that she had been before – the Mina that Jonathan loved. She had been saved.

Questions

Questions on each chapter

1 Castle Dracula
1 Where was Jonathan Harker at the beginning of the story?
2 What did the hotel keeper's wife give him?
3 Where did the carriage take him?
4 How did he know that there were wolves near him?
5 What had Jonathan brought to Count Dracula?
6 Where could Jonathan *not* go in the castle?
7 What had Mr Hawkins done for Count Dracula?
8 What could Jonathan *not* see in his looking glass?
9 What did Dracula do with the looking glass?
10 How far was it from the window to the ground?

2 The three women
1 Who was doing the servants' work in the castle?
2 What did Dracula want to send to a town in England?
3 Which town did Jonathan suggest?
4 What did Dracula tell Jonathan to write?
5 What did Jonathan see from the window?
6 What fell from Jonathan's neck?
7 Why did Jonathan lie down?
8 Which girl knelt beside him?
9 What did Jonathan feel then?
10 Until when must the girls not touch Jonathan?

3 Vampires!
1 What were the gipsies doing?
2 What happened to Jonathan's clothes?
3 How did Jonathan climb down to Dracula's room?
4 What was in the older box?
5 Why didn't Jonathan go out through the great door?
6 How did Dracula leave the castle?

4 *Mina and Lucy*
    1 What was Jack Seward's work?
    2 What arrived on the strange ship besides the boxes?
    3 Where did Mina see Lucy?
    4 What did Mina see on Lucy's neck?
    5 Who wrote a letter to Mina?
    6 Where did the madman Renfield go?
    7 Whose help did Dr Seward want?

5 *Professor Van Helsing*
    1 Who came to see Lucy at Hillingdon?
    2 Who gave blood to save Lucy?
    3 What were the white flowers?
    4 Where did Van Helsing rub the flowers?
    5 How did Mrs Westenra spoil Lucy's protection?

6 *The fight for Lucy's life*
    1 Where did Dr Seward spend (a) his days and (b) his nights?
    2 What men did Renfield attack?
    3 What happened to the blood from Dr Seward's wound?
    4 Why did Dr Hennessey go to Hillingdon?
    5 What happened to delay the telegram?
    6 What happened to Lucy's ring of garlic flowers?
    7 What did Van Helsing not allow Arthur to do?

7 *Lucy is a vampire!*
    1 What happened to the young children?
    2 Which vampire drank the children's blood?
    3 What was inside Lucy's coffin?
    4 What were Lucy's teeth like?
    5 How could they kill the vampire?

8 *Lucy's soul is saved*
    1 What did Van Helsing use when he closed Lucy's tomb?
    2 What are the "Un-Dead"?
    3 How did Van Helsing protect Arthur?
    4 Why did Van Helsing (a) pick out some of the bread and then (b) put it back?
    5 Who drove the piece of wood into Lucy's heart?
    6 What else did they do to Lucy's body?

9 *Dracula's house*
    1 Why had Jonathan told nobody except Mina his story?
    2 Who told the others about Carfax House?
    3 How many boxes did they find in the church?
    4 What attacked the four men?
    5 Why must they go back the next day?

10 *Dracula attacks Mina*
    1 Why did Dr Hennessey write down the carters' names?
    2 What happened to Renfield?
    3 Who opened the door of Mina's room? How?
    4 What was Dracula forcing Mina to do?
    5 What caused Dracula to leave the room?

11 *The end of Dracula*
    1 What did Mina's dreams tell them about Dracula?
    2 Which ship was Dracula on?
    3 What could save Mina?
    4 Where did Dracula's box leave the ship?
    5 How did Jonathan and Arthur begin their journey?
    6 How did Dr Seward go?
    7 Who went by train to Veresti and by carriage from there?
    8 Why could Mina not leave the circle round the fire?
    9 How did Van Helsing drive the vampire women away?
    10 Who were taking Dracula to his castle?
    11 How did the four friends open the box?
    12 What had Van Helsing prepared?
    13 What happened in the end to Dracula's body?
    14 What, for Mina, was the result of his death?

Questions on the whole story

These are harder questions. Read the Introduction, and think hard about the questions before you answer them. Some of them ask for your opinion, and there is no fixed answer.

1 When was a vampire active, and when could it not move?

2 What was the result when a vampire sucked a person's blood? Give an example.

3 What was the result when a person drank a vampire's blood? Give an example.

4 Give examples of Van Helsing's use of:
   a a cross
   b garlic flowers
   c the name of God
   d blessed bread

5 Jonathan Harker:
   a Why did he go to Castle Dracula at the beginning of the story?
   b What do we know about how he left Castle Dracula? How much can we guess?
   c What do we learn about his character at the end of the story?

6 Arthur Holmewood:
   a Why is he important in the story?
   b What is your opinion of his character?

7 Mina Murray:
   a What do we know about her at the beginning of the story?
   b Van Helsing "liked this young woman who knew what to do at difficult moments" (page 49). What is your opinion of her?
   c What is the end of the story for her? Does it please you?

8 What is your opinion of Dr Jack Seward's character? Why?

9 Professor Van Helsing. Try to give examples of:
   a his special knowledge and understanding of vampires
   b his courage and quick thinking

New words

bat
a flying mouselike animal that is active at night

burst
explode

castle
a large strongly built building made to be defended against attack

coffin
the box in which a dead person is put into the ground or into a tomb

Count
part of the name of a man of an important family

drip
fall, one drop after another

funeral
the solemn act of putting a dead person's body into the ground or into a tomb

garlic
a plant with white flowers and with root parts that give a strong taste in cooking, often used in the past as a medicine

ghost
a person who is dead but who appears again

gipsy
a member of a dark-haired race (perhaps of Indian origin), often travelling from place to place in Europe, earning money by making baskets, buying and selling horses and other things, playing music, etc

mist
low cloud, or masses of small drops of water in the air

myth
an ancient story, usually connected with religion or magic

scream
a very loud cry of fear or anger

shave
take all the hair from a man's face with something sharp (a razor)

shock
a sudden unpleasant
surprise. In a **state of shock**
one cannot think clearly.

telegram
words (in signals, not
spoken) sent by electricity
along wires

tomb
a place built to put a dead
body in

vampire
(in the book) a person who
drinks blood from the neck
of a living person. See also
the Introduction.